W9-CBK-868

DISCARD

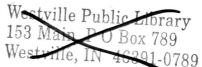
Westville Public Library
153 Main PO Box 789
Westville, IN 46391-0789

A Note to Parents

Welcome to REAL KIDS READERS, a series of phonics-based books for children who are beginning to read. In the classroom, educators use phonics to teach children how to sound out unfamiliar words, providing a firm foundation for reading skills. At home, you can use REAL KIDS READERS to reinforce and build on that foundation, because the books follow the same basic phonic guidelines that children learn in school.

Of course the best way to help your child become a good reader is to make the experience fun—and REAL KIDS READERS do that, too. With their realistic story lines and lively characters, the books engage children's imaginations. With their clean design and sparkling photographs, they provide picture clues that help new readers decipher the text. The combination is sure to entertain young children and make them truly want to read.

REAL KIDS READERS have been developed at three distinct levels to make it easy for children to read at their own pace.

- LEVEL 1 is for children who are just beginning to read.
- LEVEL 2 is for children who can read with help.
- LEVEL 3 is for children who can read on their own.

A controlled vocabulary provides the framework at each level. Repetition, rhyme, and humor help increase word skills. Because children can understand the words and follow the stories, they quickly develop confidence. They go back to each book again and again, increasing their proficiency and sense of accomplishment, until they're ready to move on to the next level. The result is a rich and rewarding experience that will help them develop a lifelong love of reading.

To Sarah, Emily, Elizabeth, Laura,
and the real Bud
—C. S.

Special thanks to FAO Schwarz for providing toys, to The Gap
for providing clothing, to Gloria's Kids Beds for providing the
bed, and to Callie R. C. Smith and Julianna Carlson.

Produced by DWAI / Seventeenth Street Productions, Inc.
Reading Specialist: Virginia Grant Clammer

Copyright © 1998 by The Millbrook Press, Inc. All rights reserved. Published by
The Millbrook Press, Inc. Printed in the United States of America.

Real Kids Readers and the Real Kids Readers logo are trademarks of The Millbrook Press, Inc.

Library of Congress Cataloging-in-Publication Data

Simon, Charnan.
  The good bad day / Charnan Simon ; photographs by Dorothy Handelman.
      p.   cm. — (Real kids readers. Level 2)
  Summary: Pam is sick and having a very bad day until her parents and her friend help to
cheer her up.
  ISBN 0-7613-2017-2 (lib. bdg.). — ISBN 0-7613-2042-3 (pbk.)
  [1. Sick—Fiction.] I. Handelman, Dorothy, ill. II. Title. III. Series.
PZ7.S6035Go 1998
[E]—dc21   98-10043
                                                                        CIP
                                                                        AC

pbk: 10 9 8 7 6 5 4 3 2 1
lib: 10 9 8 7 6 5 4 3 2 1

The Good Bad Day

By Charnan Simon

Photographs by Dorothy Handelman

M

The Millbrook Press

Brookfield, Connecticut

It was a bad day.
The sky was gray.
The air was cold.
Pam felt hot.
Her nose was stuffed up.
Her head hurt.

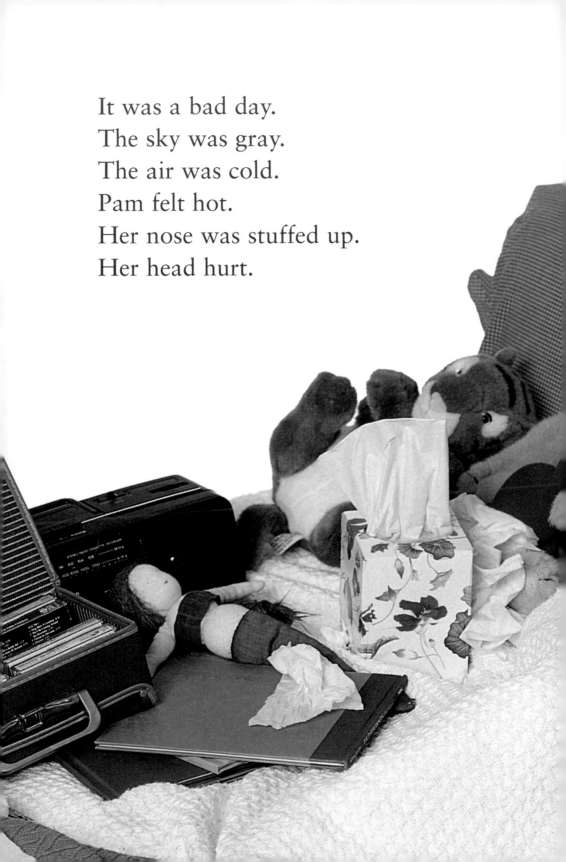

Pam had a bad cold.
She had to stay home,
and her friend Jill
could not come and play.
That made Pam mad.

"I hate to be sick," she told Teddy.
"It is no fun!"

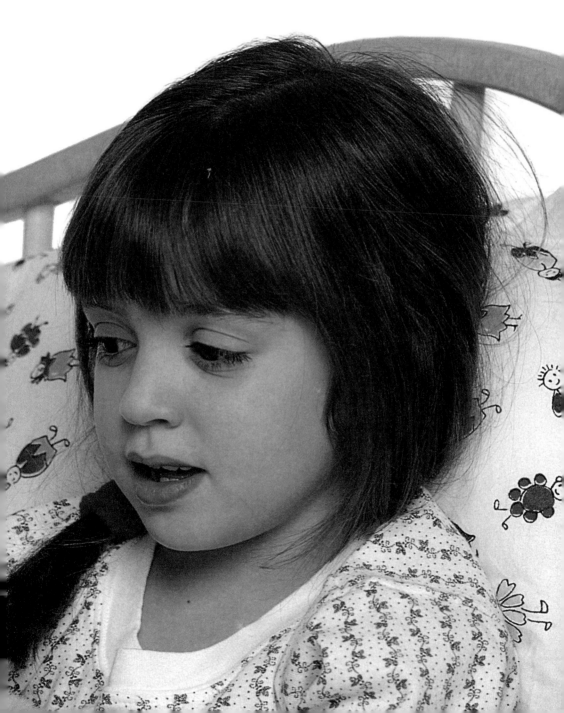

Pam got out of bed.
She picked out a book
and tried to read.
The boy in the book
was playing in the snow.
He was having fun.
Pam was not!
She closed that book—fast.

Pam got out her art stuff.
She tried to draw her cat, Bud.
"Sit still, Bud!" she said.

But Bud did not sit still.
He ran away.
Bad cat!

Pam played a tape.
The first song was
"Put on a Happy Face."
Pam did not want to do that.
She put on a mad face.
That was the face for her!

Pam got back into bed.
She curled up in a little ball.
She felt mad and sad and sick.
Dad was at work.
Mom was downstairs.
Jill was at her house.
"No one loves me," she told Teddy.
Then she cried herself to sleep.

When Pam woke up,
the house was still.
She felt all alone.

But wait!
What was that noise?

It was Mom with a tray.
There was a rose on the tray.
It was red and soft.
There was tea on the tray.
It was hot and sweet.
And there was toast on the tray—
toast with grape jelly.

"Yum!" said Pam.
"Grape jelly is the best."
She ate one bite.
She ate two bites.
She ate all of her toast.

Mom picked up a deck of cards.
"Let's play Go Fish," she said.
Pam and Mom
played five games of Go Fish.
Pam won all five!
Mom gave her a prize.

23

RING! RING! It was Dad calling.
He had a joke for Pam.
"Knock, knock," he said.
"Who's there?" said Pam.
"Itch," said Dad.
"Itch who?" said Pam.
"Bless you," said Dad.
It was a good joke for a girl with a cold.

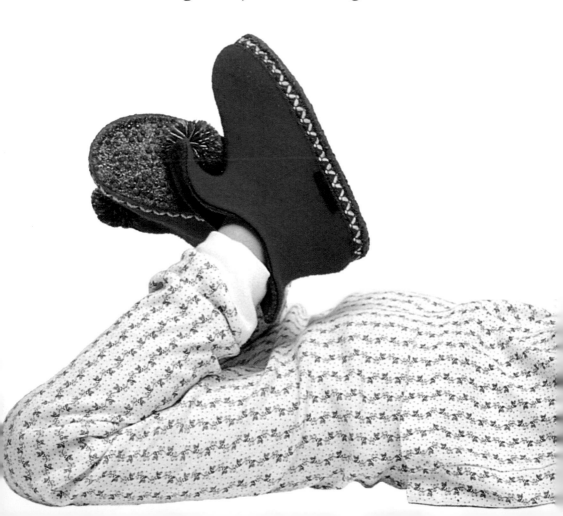

DING DONG! The doorbell rang.
Mom went to the door.
She came back with a card.
"Mail for Pam," she said.

The card was from Jill.
She had drawn two girls on it.
One was Pam. One was Jill.

Pam went to the window.
She looked down.
There was Jill!
Jill waved to Pam.
Pam waved to Jill.

Pam felt much better.
She turned on her tape.
She picked up her book.
Bud came to sit with her.
Pam was still sick.
But she was not mad or sad.
Her bad day had turned into
a good day.

Phonic Guidelines

Use the following guidelines to help your child read the words in *The Good Bad Day*.

Short Vowels
When two consonants surround a vowel, the sound of the vowel is usually short. This means you pronounce *a* as in apple, *e* as in egg, *i* as in igloo, *o* as in octopus, and *u* as in umbrella. Short-vowel words in this story include: *bad, bed, Bud, but, cat, Dad, did, fun, got, had, hot, lap, mad, Mom, not, Pam, ran, red, sad, sit, yum.*

Consonant Blends
When two or more different consonants are side by side, they usually blend to make a combined sound. In this story, short-vowel words with consonant blends include: *best, bless, ding, dong, fast, felt, itch, rang, ring, song, stuff, went.*

Double Consonants
When two identical consonants appear side by side, one of them is silent. In this story, double consonants appear in the short-vowel words *Jill, still, stuffed,* and in the *all*-family words: *all, ball, calling.*

R-Controlled Vowels
When a vowel is followed by the letter *r,* its sound is changed by the *r.* In this story, words with r-controlled vowels include: *air, art, card, curled, first, for, girl, her, hurt, turned, work.*

Long Vowel and Silent E
If a word has a vowel and ends with an *e,* usually the vowel is long and the *e* is silent. Long vowels are pronounced the same way as their alphabet names. In this story, words with a long vowel and silent *e* include: *ate, bite, came, closed, face, five, gave, grape, hate, home, joke, made, nose, prize, rose, tape, waved, woke.*

Double Vowels
When two vowels are side by side, usually the first vowel is long and the second vowel is silent. Double-vowel words in this story include: *day, gray, mail, play, read, sleep, stay, sweet, tea, toast, tray, wait.*

Diphthongs
Sometimes when two vowels (or a vowel and a consonant) are side by side, they combine to make a diphthong—a sound that is different from long or short vowel sounds. Diphthongs are: *au/aw, ew, oi/oy, ou/ow.* In this story, words with diphthongs include: *boy, down, draw, house, noise.*

Consonant Digraphs
Sometimes when two different consonants are side by side, they make a digraph that represents a single new sound. Consonant digraphs are: *ch, sh, th, wh.* In this story, words with digraphs include: *fish, much, that, then, there, what, when, who, with.*

Silent Consonants
Sometimes when two different consonants appear side by side, one of them is silent. In this story, words with silent consonants include: *back, deck, knock, sick.*

Sight Words
Sight words are those words that a reader must learn to recognize immediately—by sight—instead of by sounding them out. They occur with high frequency in easy texts. Sight words not included in the above categories are: *a, and, at, be, come, could, do, from, go, good, I, in, into, is, it, little, me, no, of, on, one, out, put, said, she, the, to, up, was, you.*

Westville Public Library
153 Main, P.O. Box 789
Westville, IN 46391-0789

#16.90

*

E
SIM

Simon, Charnan.
The good bad day

Date Due			
P 1 '99			
MY 12 '99			
JE 23 '99			
AG 17 '99			
MAR 04 2003			
APR 05 2005			
JUL 1 4 2005			

DISCARD

Westville Public Library
153 Main, P.O. Box 789
Westville, IN 46391-0789